WORLD WAR I

WORLD WAR I
THE GREAT WAR BEGINS

Ruijie Zhou

gatekeeper press
Tampa, Florida

The content associated with this book is the sole work and responsibility of the author. Gatekeeper Press had no involvement in the generation of this content.

Copyright for the illustration: iStockphoto.com/johnnyknez (The Great War scene)

World War I: The Great War Begins

Published by Gatekeeper Press

7853 Gunn Hwy., Suite 209
Tampa, FL 33626

www.GatekeeperPress.com

Copyright © 2024 by Ruijie Zhou

All rights reserved. Neither this book, nor any parts within it may be sold or reproduced in any form or by any electronic or mechanical means, including information storage and retrieval systems, without permission in writing from the author. The only exception is by a reviewer, who may quote short excerpts in a review.

ISBN (hardcover): 9781662941856

ISBN (paperback): 9781662941863

eISBN: 9781662941870

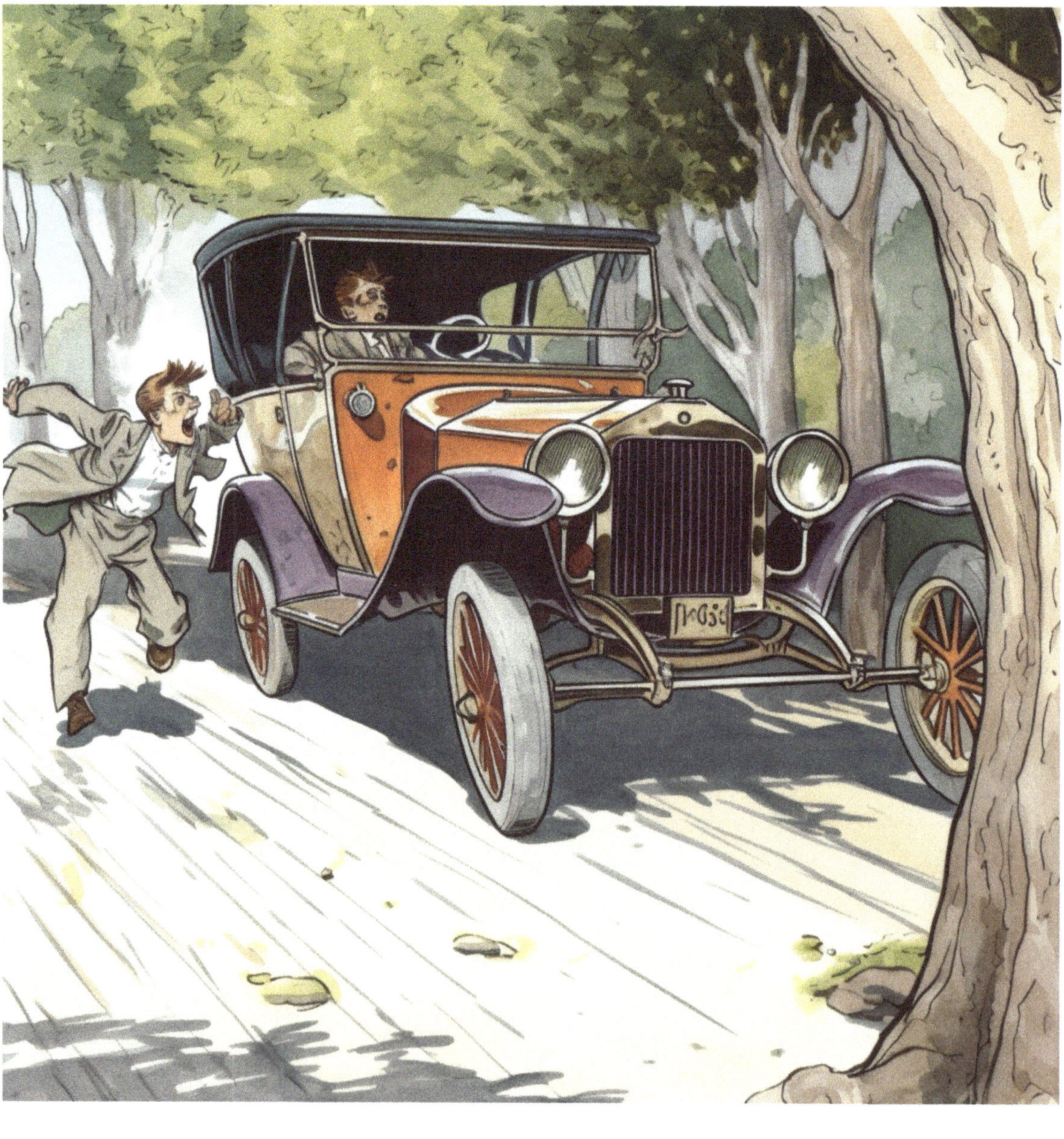

Causes of the War

Before the war started a Serbian killer came to Austria-Hungary to look for the heir-apparent, Archduke Franz Ferdinand. The first time the killer failed, but the second time he succeeded, causing World War I, or WWI. Then countries started to form alliances to fight against the Central Power. The most famous alliances were Austria-Hungary, Germany, and the Ottoman Empire, known as the Central Powers, because they were in the middle of Europe. Another alliance was Russia, Japan, Italy, the US, and the United Kingdom.

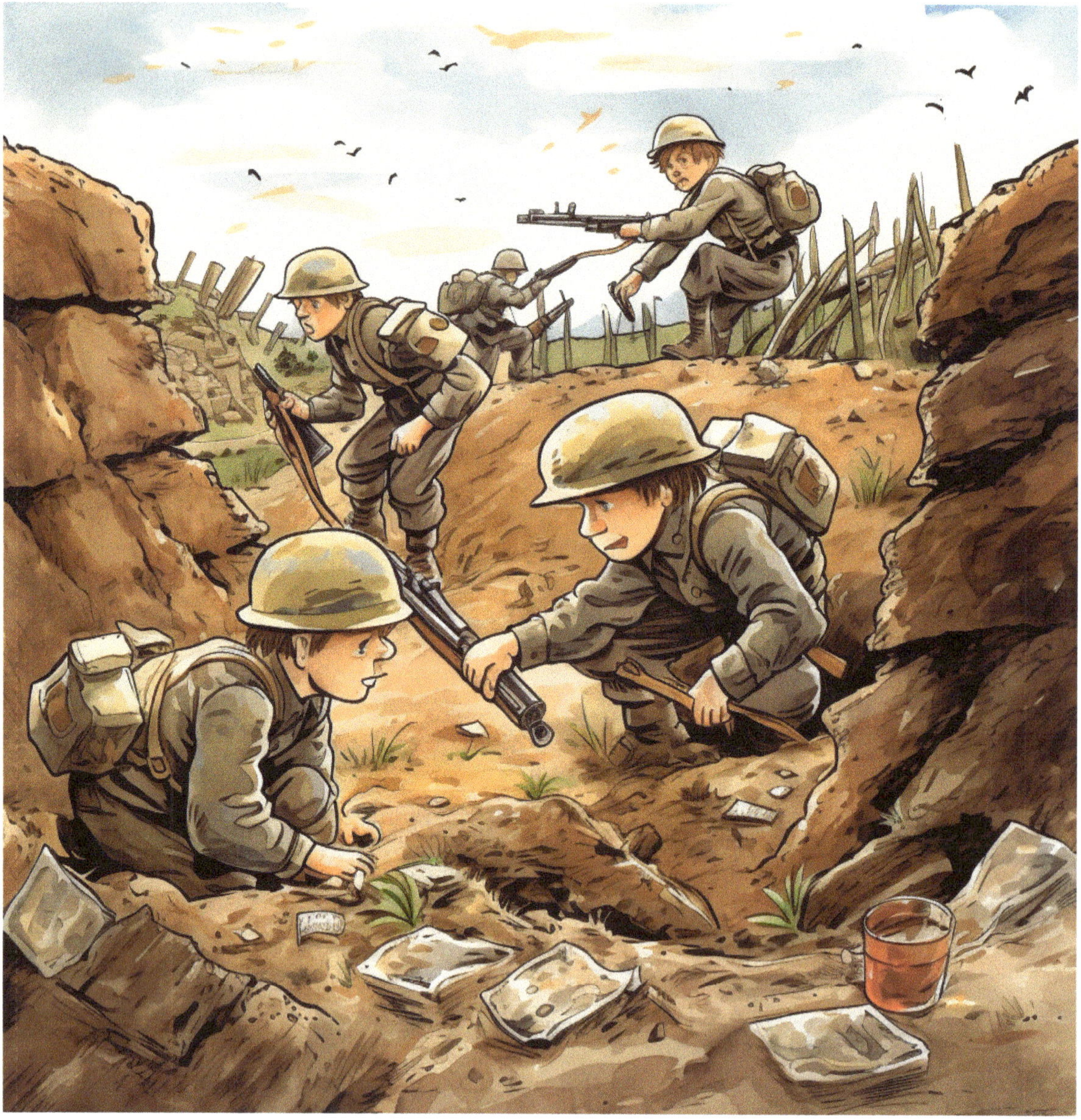

Life in the Trenches

Soldiers lived in trenches, which is a type of defensive method in battlefields to protect the soldiers during battle. Trenches were often dirty and had a lot of rats and bugs crawling around, which made soldiers sick. Planes would also drop bombs on the trenches.

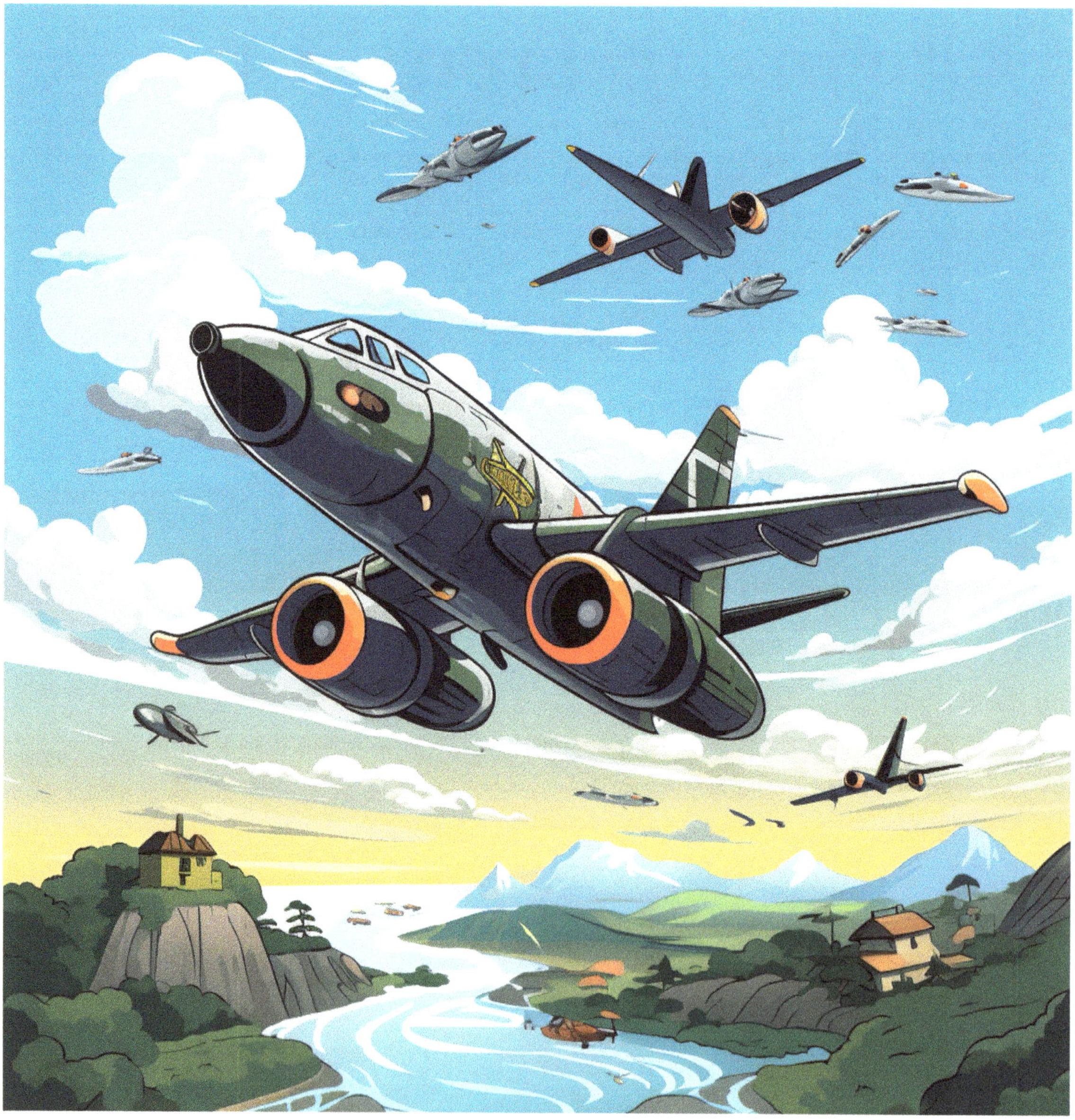

New Weapons

During WWI, we saw new versions of weapons, including: rifles, pistols, tanks, battleships, and land mines. These weapons were designed to kill and destroy enemies. Even though this was a war, there were still rules to follow. For example, there were bans on certain weapons. The Central Power Some of these countries did not care about the rules. They used illegal weapons like toxic gas, which can make a person sick, or even die.

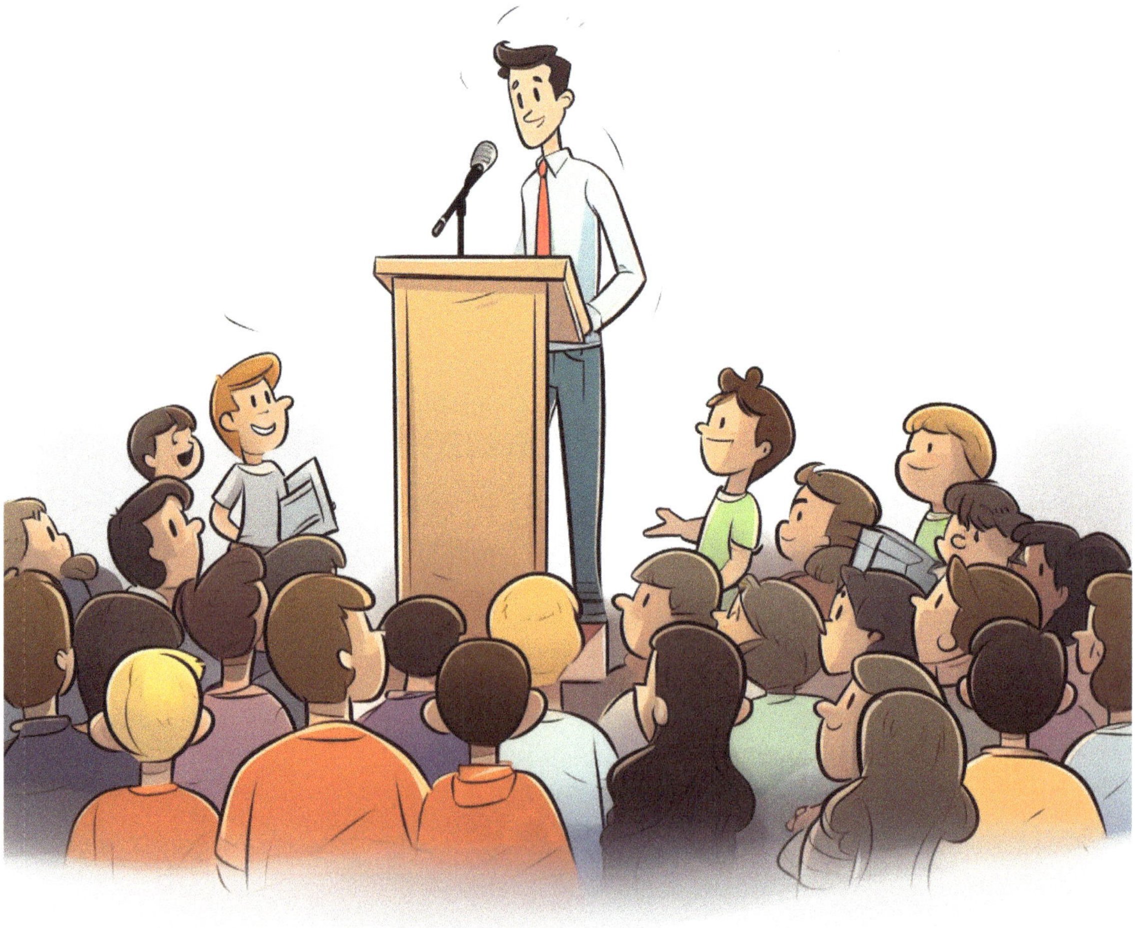

Important Leaders

In WWI, there were famous leaders. One was Woodrow Wilson, who was the 28th president of the United States of America. He was famous for declaring war on the Central Powers. Another is Kaiser Wilhelm II. He was the leader of Germany during the war. He is famous for his assurance of unlimited support to Austria-Hungary. And lastly, General John J. Pershing. He was a US general who led the first major offense against Europe.

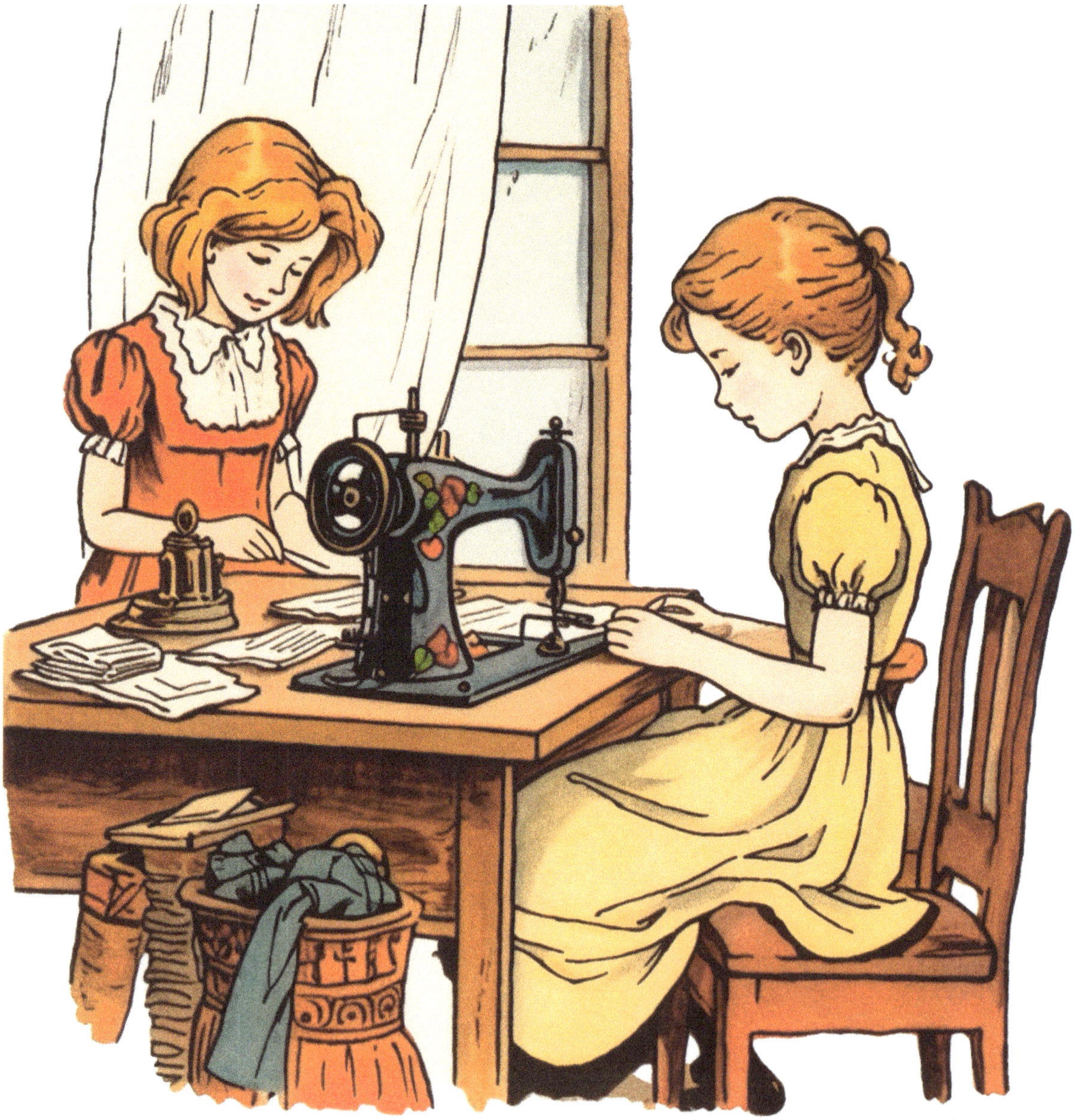

Women and the Home Front

While most men were fighting in the front of the battlefields, the women were doing jobs at home. For example, they took care of the wounded soldiers, and worked in the factories that supplied the front with supplies, like bandages, gun parts, and ammunition.

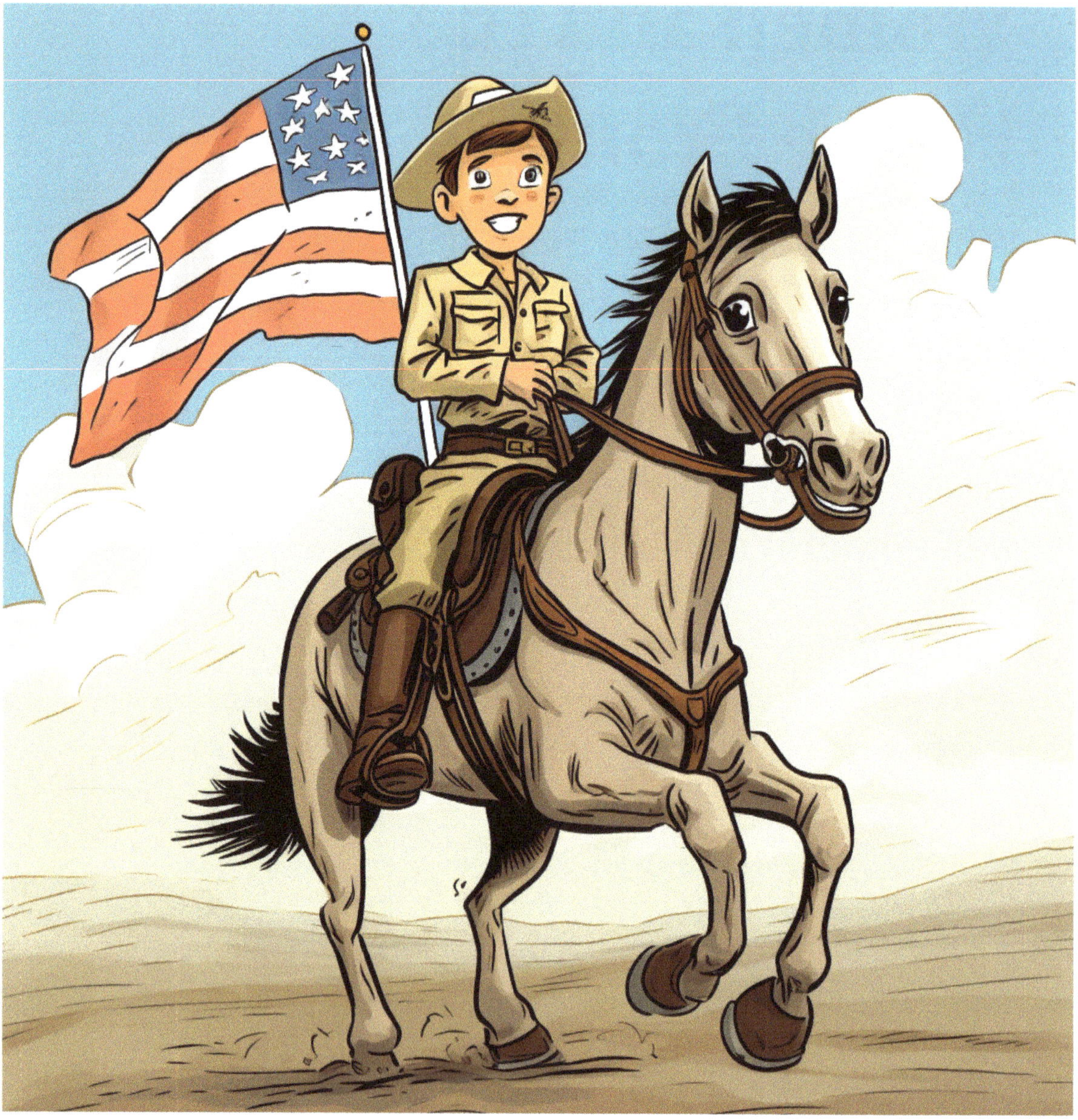

Animals in the War

Animals also played a major role in WWI. They were used to find people who were hurt, to guard prisoners, to patrol around the trenches, and sometimes to attack enemies. The animals used most frequently on the field were dogs, horses, and pigeons.

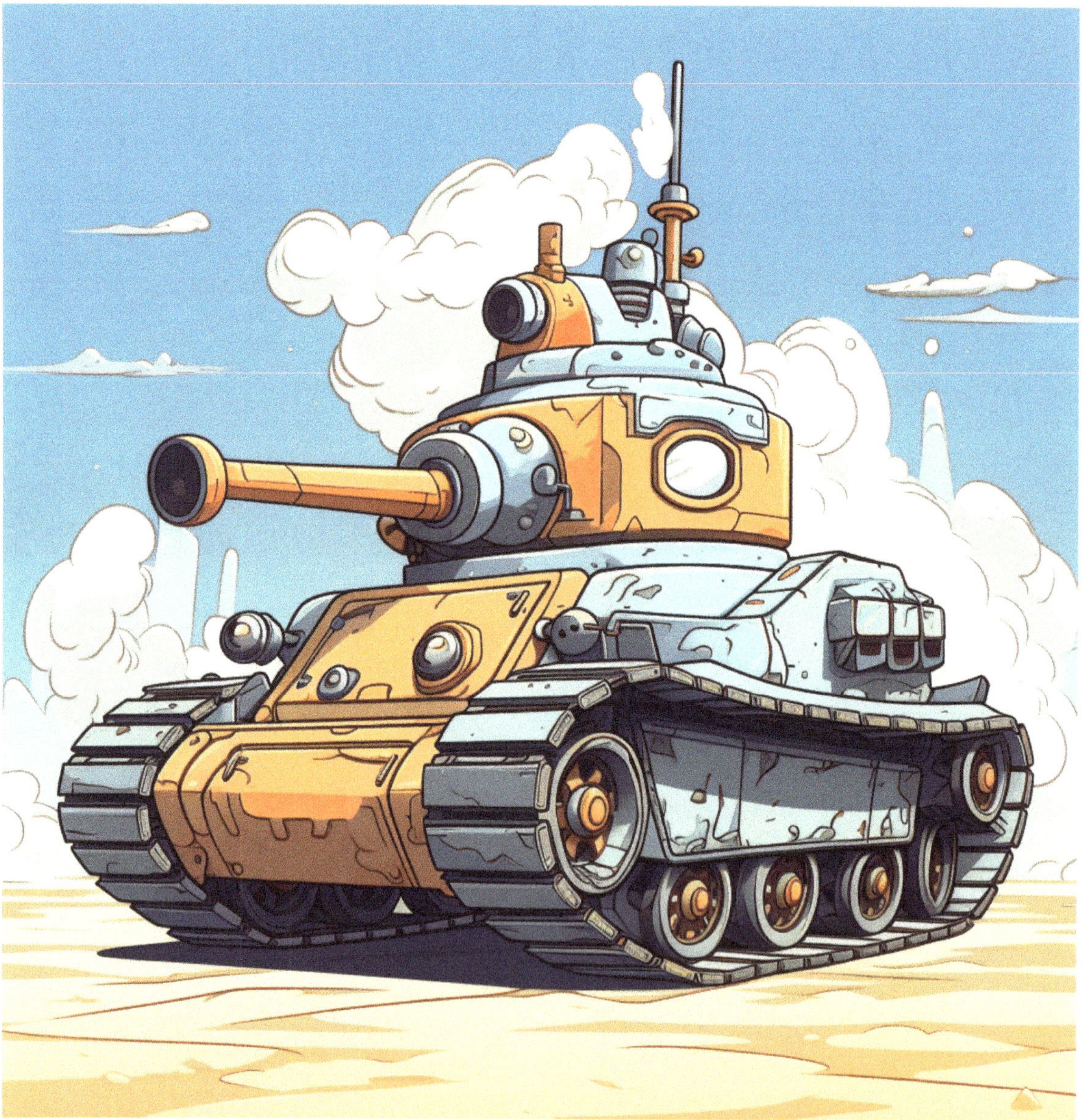

Major Battles

The key battles during the war are the Battle of the Somme and the Battle of Verdun. The Battle of the Somme was the first battle where tanks were used in combat. The Battle of Verdun was the longest-lasting battle in WWI and one of the costliest ones.

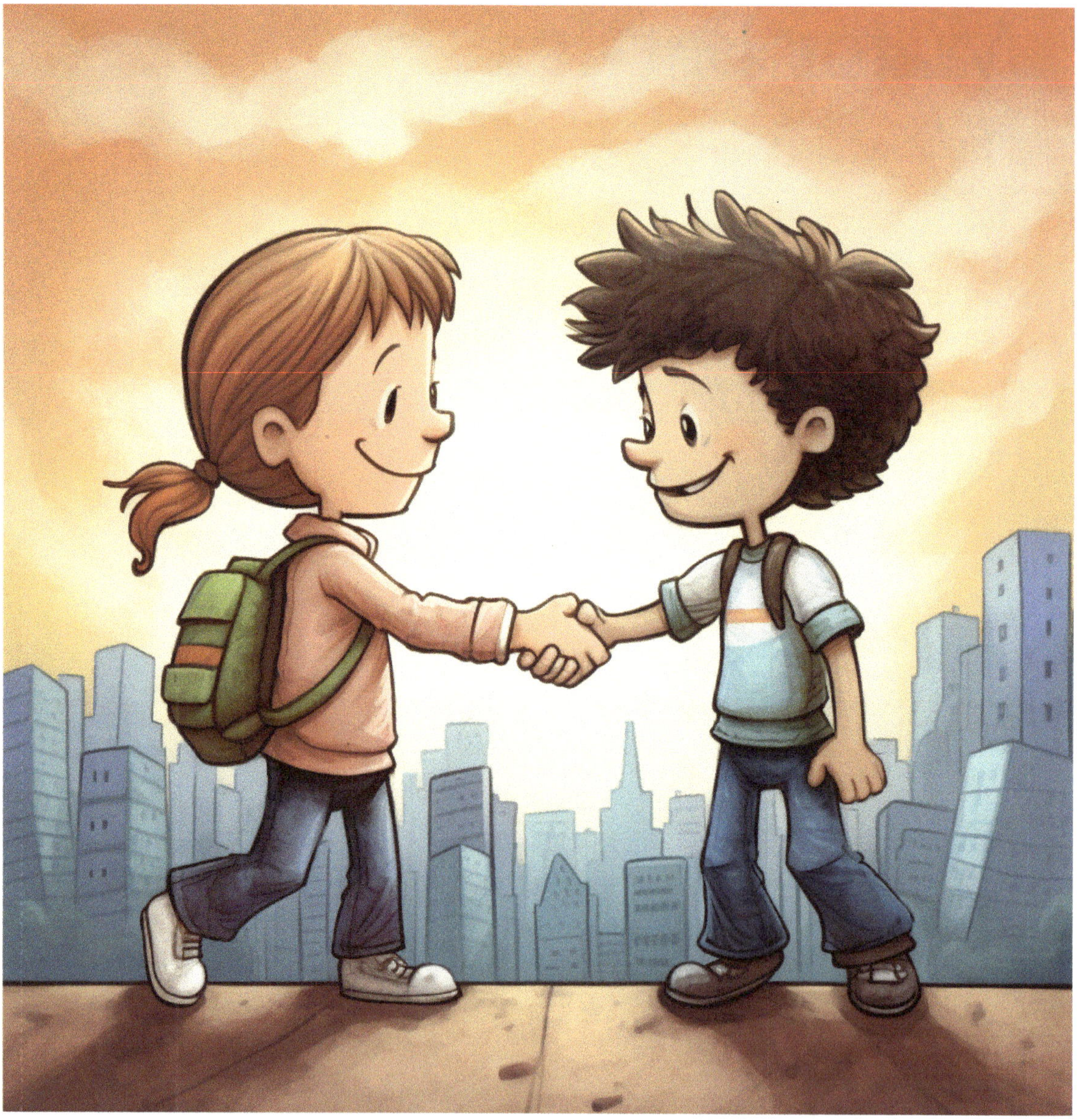

The End of the War

The war ended on November 11, 1918, when the Allies defeated the Germans at the Battle of Mons. The Allies took land from Germany and new countries formed after WWI, including Poland. Most of the Central Powers lost land and became different countries. As an example, the Ottoman empire became what is now known as Turkey.

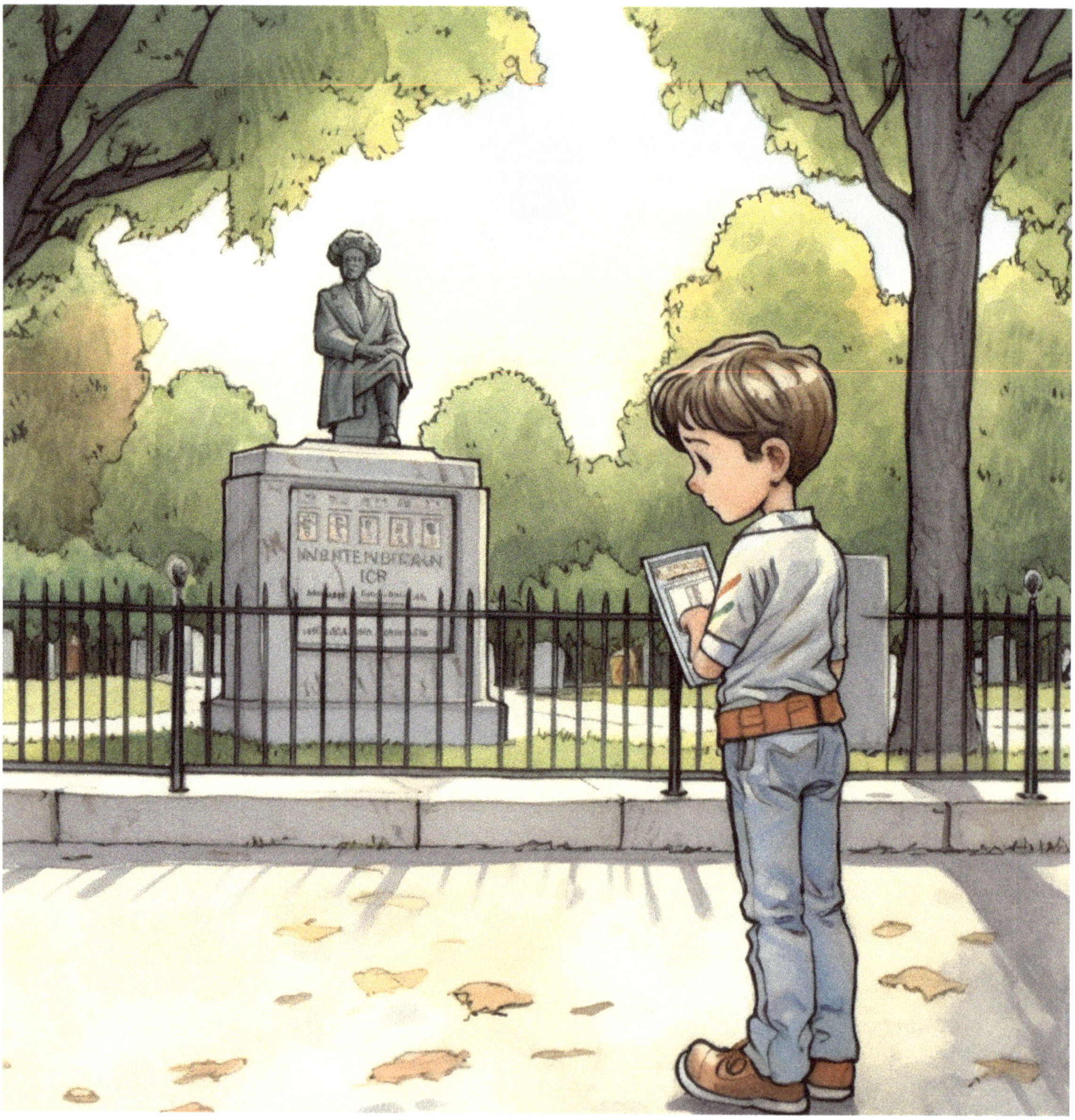

Remembering the Fallen

We respect lives lost wars by setting up memorials honoring the people who died. You can find a memorial park anywhere, where you can see the soldier's names carved in stone. Each year we have a day to remember the death of the soldiers, which is called Veterans Day.

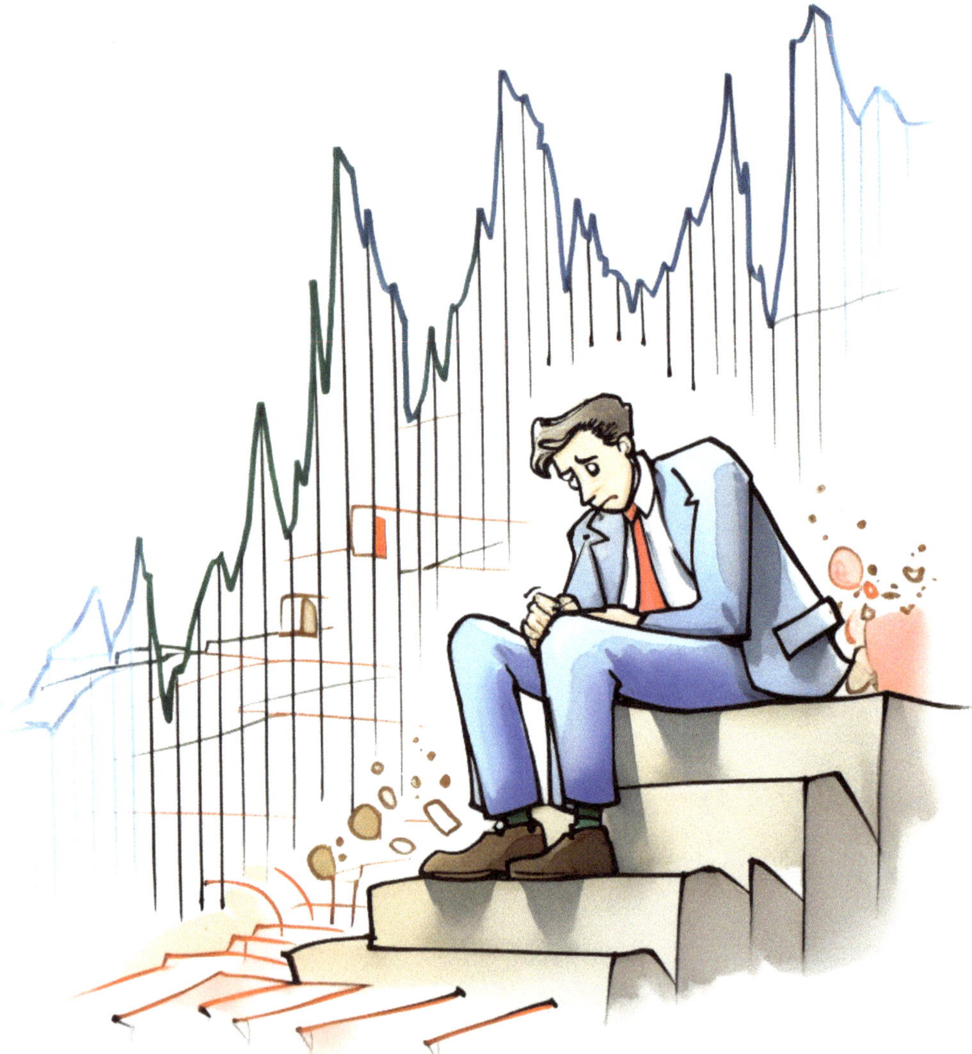

Legacy and Lessons

A lasting effect of WWI was the huge impact on the Axis's economy, politics, and land borders. After war the soldiers who survived were affected. A benefit of the war was having more advanced technology.

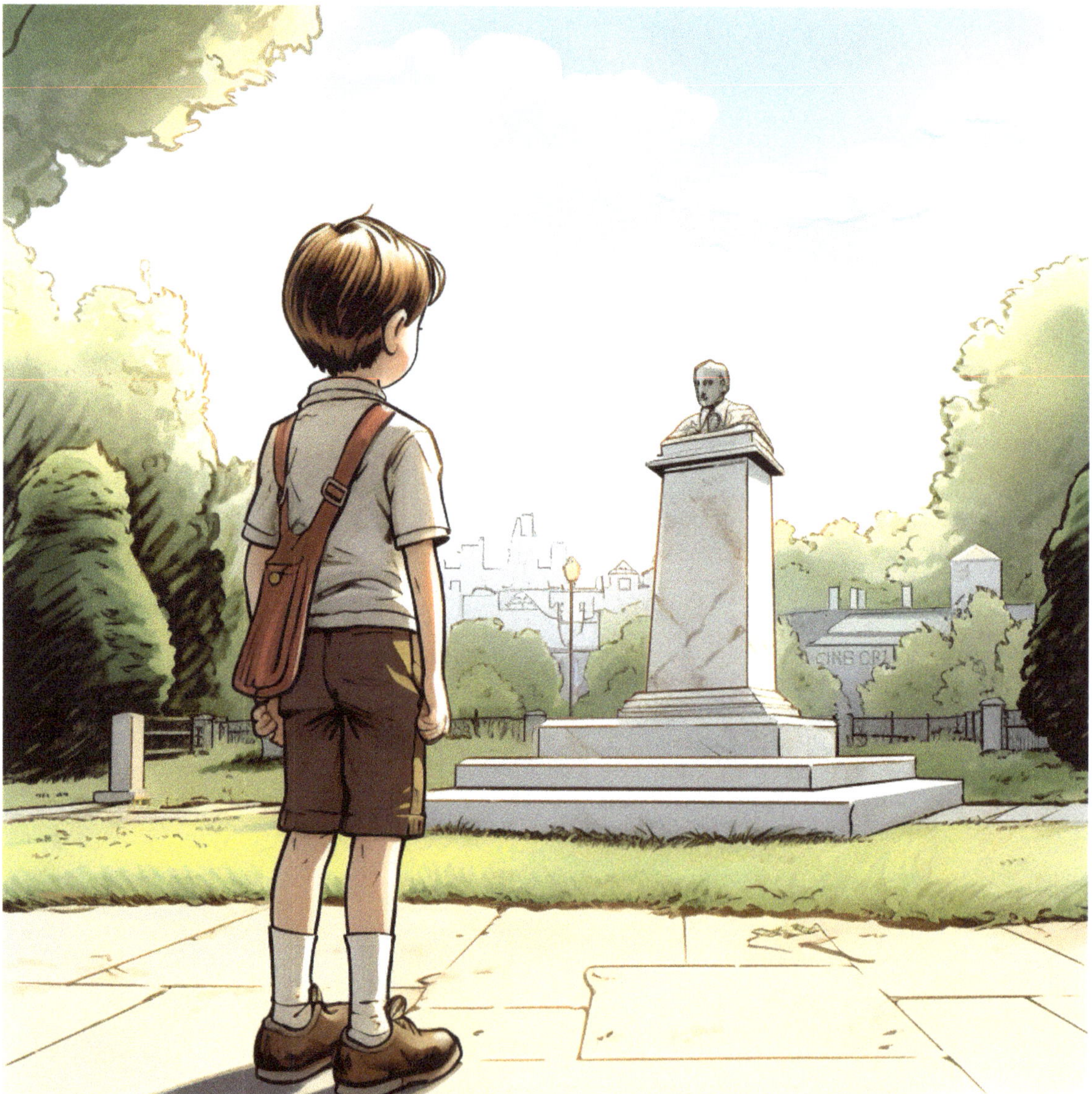

Heroes and Stories

One of the first people to introduce artificial limbs to soldiers in WWI was Jules Amar. Artificial limbs could help soldiers replace limbs if they were wounded. Because the medical conditions were not safe then, if your arm became infected, it had to be amputated. So, an artificial limb was how they replaced the soldier's arm or leg. During the war, there were a lot of actions elsewhere some people from Africa, China, and the Caribbean also aided the Allies during the war.

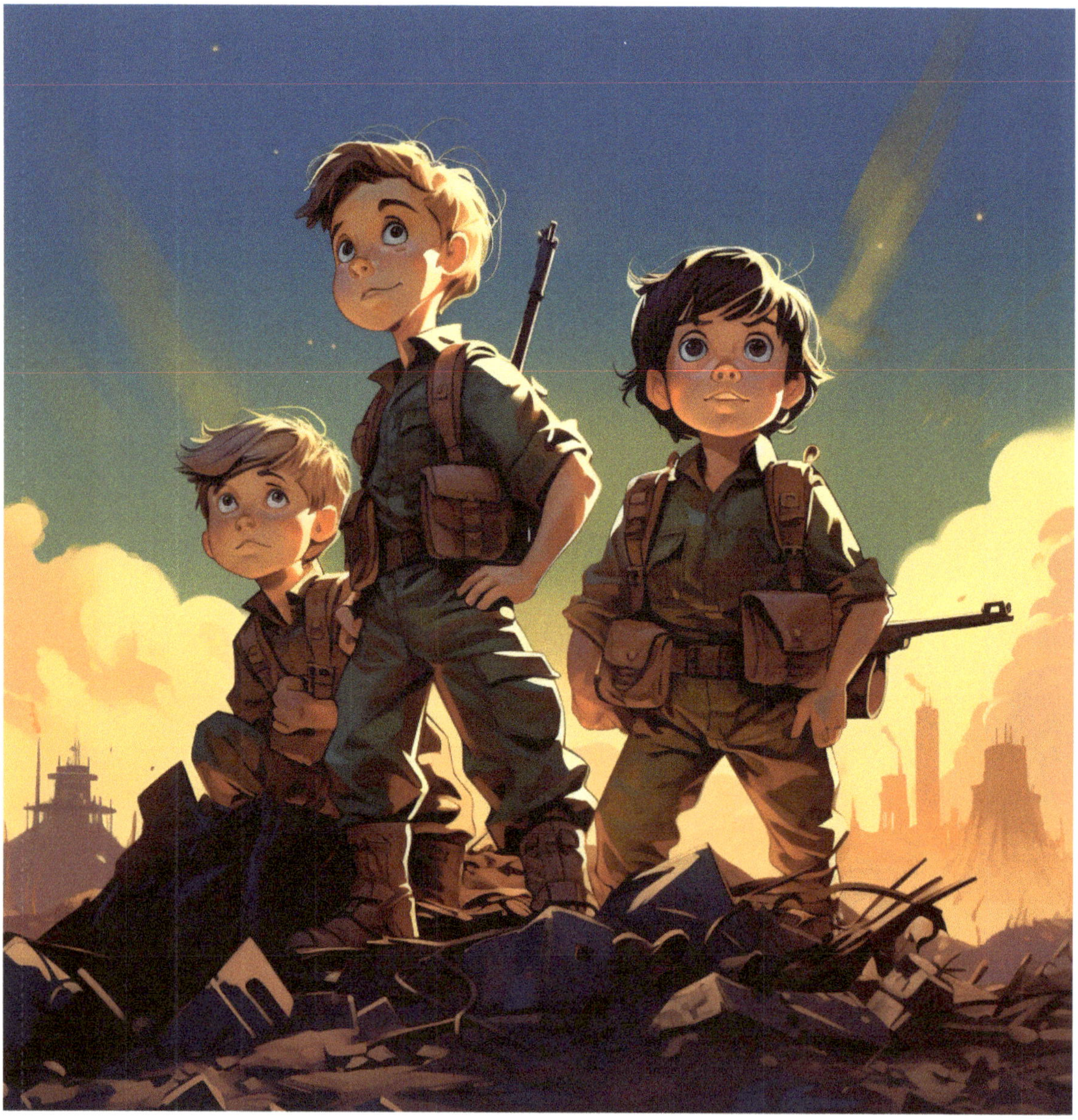

Children and the War

Children enlisted in the army, working around the age restriction. Now they would check your background more carefully before letting you join the army. There were also children used as messengers in WWI to spy for their country because they were less likely to be seen as a threat.

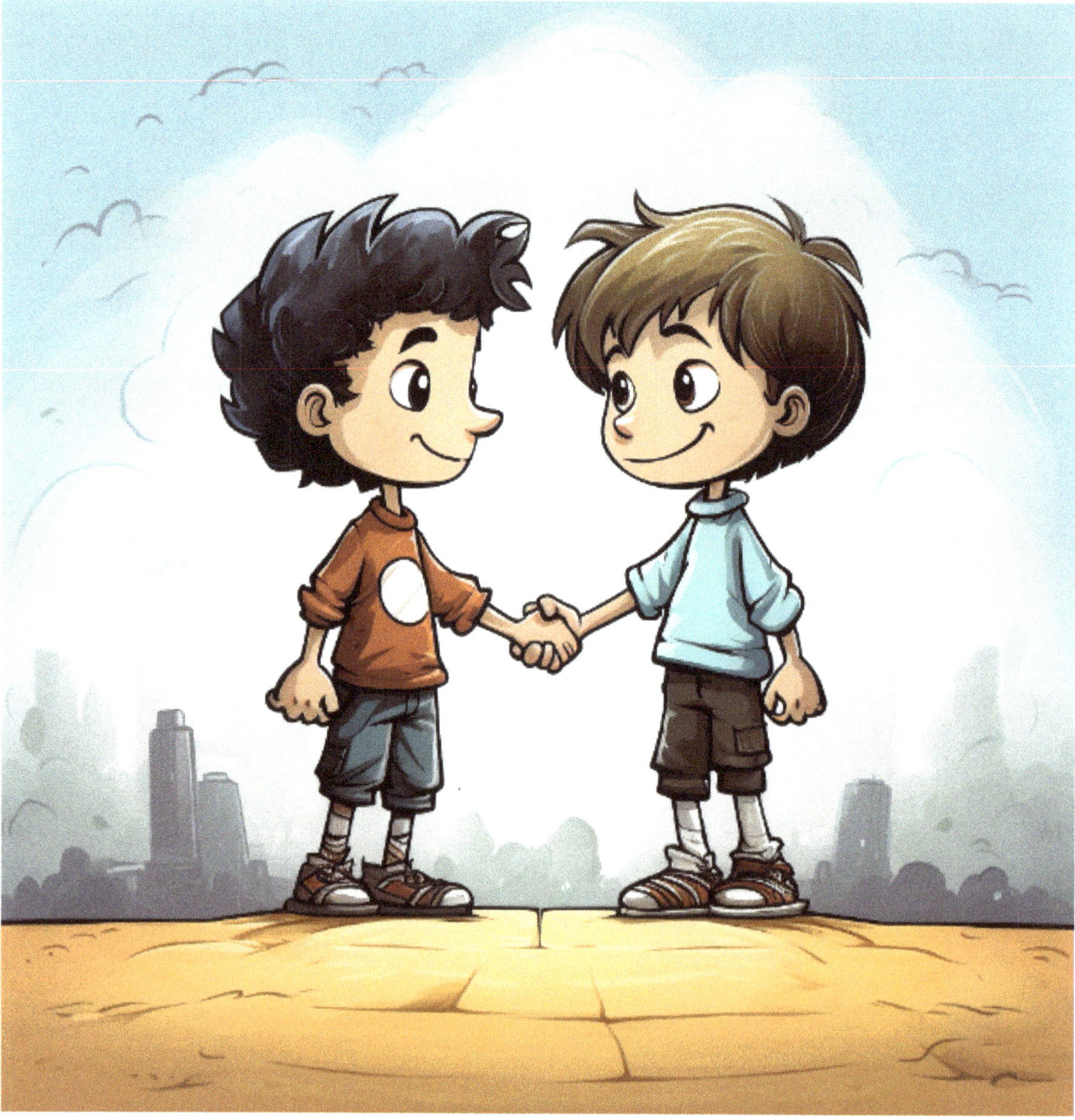

Peace and Hope

After the war, the Germans were forced to sign a treaty called the Treaty of Versailles. As a result, Germany had to give up a lot of money and needed to reduce their air force soldier number to 100,000 soldiers from 500,000.